Adapted from the Curious George film series
edited by Margret Rey and Alan J. Shalleck

1 9 8 8

Houghton Mifflin Company, Boston

*Library of Congress Cataloging-in-Publication Data*

Curious George goes to the amusement park/edited by Margret Rey and
Alan J. Shalleck.
p. cm.
"Adapted from the Curious George film series."
Summary: The amusement park customers are delighted when Curious
George gets into the ticket seller's booth.
ISBN 0-395-48665-3
[1. Monkeys–Fiction. 2. Amusement parks–Fiction.] I. Rey,
Margret. II. Shalleck, Alan J. III. Curious George goes to the
amusement park (Motion picture)
PZ7.C92169 1988 88-14757
[E]–dc19 CIP
AC



Printed in the United States of America

Y 10 9 8 7 6 5 4 3 2 1

"I know what we can do today, George,"
said the man with the yellow hat.
"Let's go to the amusement park."

When they arrived at the park, they saw
their friends Yvonne and her aunt Ruby.

"George, you get the tickets while I park the car," said the man.

The ticket booth was closed,
but a side window was open just enough for
a little monkey to get in!

Inside the booth, a lever was sticking up
from the counter. George was curious. What was it for?

He pulled the lever. A roll of tickets popped up
and the window opened.

Children came running from everywhere.
Yvonne was the first in line.

"Hi, George," she said. "All I have is one dollar.
How many tickets can I get?"

George pressed a button and out came the tickets.
"Wow," Yvonne said happily.
"Aunt Ruby will be surprised!"

Yvonne and everybody in line got
free tickets from George.

Finally, the real ticket seller appeared.
"What's going on?" he cried.
"Who's inside that booth?"

He ran to the door and unlocked it.
"A monkey! How dare you give away my tickets for free!"

George was scared. He quickly escaped
through the window.

“Guards!” shouted the ticket seller.
“Stop that monkey!”

A guard and the ticket seller ran after George.

But George had disappeared into the crowd.
He ducked into the House of Mirrors.

How funny he looked! First tall, then short, then fat.

Then the owner came along and chased George out.
He had no ticket.

Next George went over to the roller coaster.
Aunt Ruby and Yvonne were just coasting by!

Aunt Ruby was scared riding the roller coaster.
She threw up her arms and her purse flew through the air.

How good that George was a monkey!

When the roller coaster stopped,
Yvonne said, "That was fun!"
"Not for me," said Aunt Ruby. "I lost my purse."

Then she saw George.
"Look, George found my purse!"

"Thank you so much," she said.

Suddenly, a hand reached out and grabbed George.

"I finally found you!"
said the angry ticket seller.

"Wait," said Aunt Ruby. "Look how many children want to buy your tickets. George started that line. Besides, he found my purse."

"Well," said the ticket seller,
"I guess I'll just have to forget about it."
And he did.

Just then, the man with the yellow hat came over.
"How about a ride for everybody? I'll treat!"

So they all went on the roller coaster again.